Rosie
and the
Pre-loved Dress

Leanne Hatch

G.P. PUTNAM'S SONS

One afternoon, Rosie went with her mother to drop off donations at the local thrift shop.

As Rosie rummaged through the racks of gently worn, pre-loved clothing, something caught her eye. Nestled between a fuzzy wool sweater and a faded flannel shirt was a dress. But not just any dress.

One that sparkled and shined.
It was magical.

It would soon belong to Rosie.

Rosie could not wait to try on the new-to-her dress. When she unbuttoned the back, she discovered a name handwritten on the inside label: MILA.

Who was Mila? wondered Rosie. Who was the girl who wore the dress before her?

She imagined meeting Mila.
What would they laugh about
together?

Did Mila also like tortilla chips
in her tuna sandwich?

Did she also like
purple nail polish

and mismatched
socks?

Did she, too, like skateboarding

and origami?

Maybe Mila was a trapeze artist
soaring through the air.

Or an ice princess gliding
on a frozen lake.

Maybe she became a mermaid with a shimmery fish tail when she touched the water with her toes.

Rosie wore the dress every day.

Occasionally, Rosie even imagined herself
soaring through the air, gliding across the ice,
or flipping her tail deep in the ocean.
Until . . .

. . . the day the dress fit more like a top—
no matter how much she pulled it down—
and the sequined trim was scratchy in
ways it had never been before.

Until the day Rosie outgrew the dress.

She tried it over pants,

as room decor,

and modern art.

She tried it on her giant
stuffed giraffe, too,

before deciding that it
was someone else's turn
to love the dress just as
much as she did.

Rosie got out a permanent marker, then carefully wrote her name on the label next to Mila's. She thought about the memories she had made while wearing the dress. She thought about how Mila also had her own memories.

Even though Rosie was sad to let it go, she knew that her favorite dress had many more memories to make. So Rosie and her mother returned to the thrift store to make a very special donation.

Before leaving, Rosie searched the racks once again, only to discover the most magical pre-loved . . .

. . . purse!

For Lucy

G. P. PUTNAM'S SONS
An imprint of Penguin Random House LLC, New York

First published in the United States of America
by G. P. Putnam's Sons, an imprint of Penguin Random House LLC, 2022
Copyright © 2022 by Leanne Hatch
Penguin supports copyright. Copyright fuels creativity, encourages diverse voices, promotes free speech,
and creates a vibrant culture. Thank you for buying an authorized edition of this book and for complying with
copyright laws by not reproducing, scanning, or distributing any part of it in any form without permission.
You are supporting writers and allowing Penguin to continue to publish books for every reader.

G. P. Putnam's Sons is a registered trademark of Penguin Random House LLC.

Visit us online at penguinrandomhouse.com

Library of Congress Cataloging-in-Publication Data
Names: Hatch, Leanne, author, illustrator.
Title: Rosie and the pre-loved dress / Leanne Hatch.
Description: New York: G. P. Putnam's Sons, [2022] | Summary: Rosie finds a beautiful dress at the local thrift shop
and discovers a name handwritten on the label: Mila, who must have loved the sparkly dress as much as Rosie—and when
Rosie outgrows the dress, she adds her name to the label and returns it to the thrift shop for another girl to find and love.
Identifiers: LCCN 2021035189 (print) | LCCN 2021035190 (ebook) | ISBN 9780593354483 (hardcover) |
ISBN 9780593354490 (ebook) | ISBN 9780593354506 (kindle edition)
Subjects: LCSH: Dresses—Juvenile fiction. | Imagination—Juvenile fiction. | Thrift shops—Juvenile fiction. |
CYAC: Dresses—Fiction. | Imagination—Fiction. | Thrift shops—Fiction.
Classification: LCC PZ7.1.H3798 Ro 2022 (print) | LCC PZ7.1.H3798 (ebook) | DDC [E]—dc23
LC record available at https://lccn.loc.gov/2021035189
LC ebook record available at https://lccn.loc.gov/2021035190

Manufactured in China
ISBN 9780593354483
1 3 5 7 9 10 8 6 4 2
TOPL

Design by Suki Boynton · Text set in Sassoon Infant
The art was created digitally with hand painted textures throughout.